Russell Library
W9-AVK-632

The Mean Team from Mars

written and illustrated by
Scoular Anderson

Managing Editor: Catherine Neitge
Story Consultant: Terry Flaherty
Page Production: Melissa Kes
Creative Director: Keith Griffin
Editorial Director: Carol Jones

First American edition published in 2006 by
Picture Window Books
5115 Excelsior Boulevard
Suite 232
Minneapolis, MN 55416
1-877-845-8392
www.picturewindowbooks.com

First published in Great Britain by
A & C Black Publishers Limited
37 Soho Square, London W1D 3QZ

Printed in the United States of America.

Library of Congress Cataloging-in-Publication Data
Anderson, Scoular.
The mean team from Mars / written and illustrated by Scoular Anderson.
p. cm. — (Read-it! chapter books)
Summary: When Rory adds a disguised alien to his team, their play
is out of this world.
ISBN 1-4048-1274-1 (hard cover)
[1. Soccer—Fiction. 2. Extraterrestrial beings—Fiction.] I. Title. II. Series.
PZ7.A5495Mea 2005
[Fic]—dc22 2005007190

Table of Contents

It was Tuesday. The Arden players were training for their big match against the team from Springfield.

Rory went in to tackle and ...

Mr. Mint blew his whistle.

Rory spent the rest of the match standing on the sideline.

The next Tuesday, Rory got into trouble again ...

and again the Tuesday after that.

The following week, Rory kicked one of the other players.

Mr. Mint blew his whistle so hard it made Rory's ears rattle.

PHEEEEEEEP!

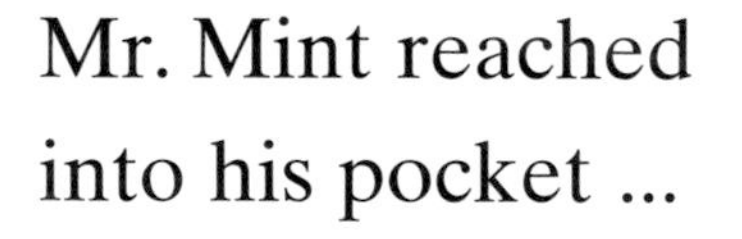

Mr. Mint reached into his pocket ...

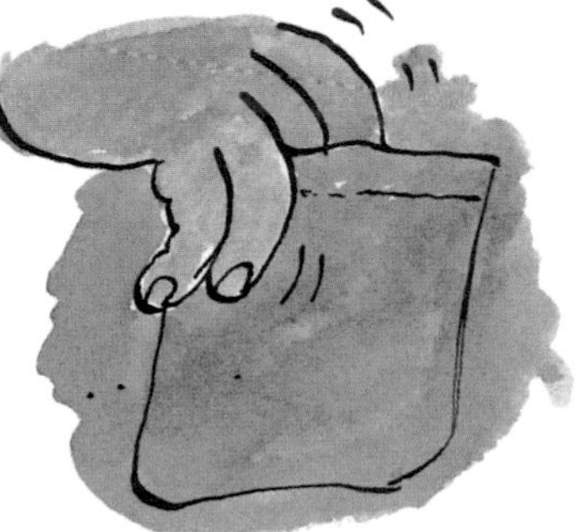

and brought out a real red card.

You're one of my best players, Rory. But you must learn to behave on the field. A red card means you get kicked off!
Sorry, Mr. Mint.
If you don't behave during the match on Saturday, you'll be off the team for good.

At last, the day of the big match came. Rory laid out his uniform on the bed.

His mom put her head in the door.

The farmer's market was busy. Rory's mom went off to buy vegetables.

Rory had saved up $20, and he looked around for something to buy.

Rory pulled out his wallet.

Rory was feeling really pleased with himself, until he met his mom.

Rory took her to the place where he had bought the quilt. But the stall wasn't there.

Back home, Rory rushed to his room with his new quilt. He had a collection of Arden United things. He had Arden United curtains ...

Arden United pens ...

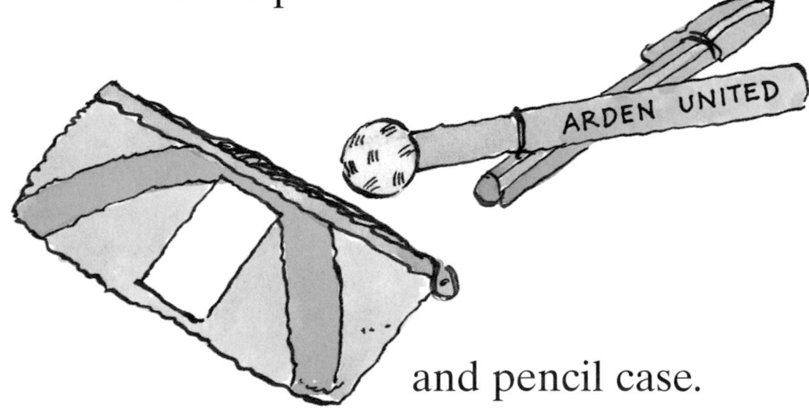

and pencil case.

He had an Arden United rug ...

and towel.

He even had
Arden United
underpants.

Now he had an Arden
United quilt.
He pulled the quilt
out of the package
and spread it on
the bed.

It was amazing. There was the Arden United field laid out in front of him.

He was very excited. He took a deep breath and jumped on to the field.

Rory didn't land on a soft quilt on top of a soft bed. His new quilt seemed to be as hard as…

Rory sat up. There was real grass under his hands and a real grandstand in front of him.

He was right in the middle of the Arden United soccer field.

There was something strange about the place. He looked up and saw what it was. The whole soccer field was covered by a glass roof.

Then he saw the date above the scoreboard.

Rory began to panic. How was he going to get back into his own time?

Rory turned round.

He saw a boy his own age, but the boy was green ...

and had four arms ...

and four legs.

Skrekie and Rory kicked the ball to one another as they ran down the field.

Are you from Earth?
Er... yes.
I'm from planet Marzipok but I've lived on Earth since I was two years old.
You're good with the ball!
So are you! We could use you on our team.

Just then, someone else came on to the field.

Mr. Migg came across to Rory.

Mr. Migg gave Rory a funny look.

I don't know about that. ... I haven't seen how you play or how you behave.
He's really good, Mr. Migg.
And I'll behave, I really will.
OK. The Mars North School will be here soon. You can play.
Yessss!

The glass roof above the stadium opened. A spaceship came through slowly. It came down and landed on the field.

The doors of the bus opened. The Mars North School team got out and walked to the changing room. Rory's eyes almost fell out of his head. If these kids were the players, he was in for a hard match.

Skrekie saw Rory stare at the visiting team.

The game began. Rory and Skrekie did well. They were small and nimble. They ran rings around the Drabonians ...

and the Plutonians ...

and even the Swurling goalie.

Then Rory had a little trouble from the Belovian.

Rory fell to the ground.

The referee blew his whistle. A big red card began to flash above the stadium.

Something very strange happened next. A long tube came down from the top of the stadium.

A voice boomed out ...

Then the Belovian was sucked up, like a piece of fluff, into a vacuum.

Just after Rory scored his third goal, the final whistle blew.

The final score came up on the scoreboard …

The teams began to walk off the field. Rory and Skrekie gave a big leap of joy.

Rory landed on something hard for the second time that day. It was his bedroom floor.

Skrekie landed on top of him.

Just then, Rory saw the time on the clock beside his bed.

Rory pointed to his Arden United calendar.

Rory clasped his knee. The tackle from the big Belovian had made it really sore.

Rory looked Skrekie up and down.

Skrekie needed a disguise. Rory thought about it.

Some of his mom's face powder made
Skrekie less green.

Skrekie hid a pair of
arms under his shirt.

Jogging pants
hid his legs well.

Skrekie's feet
werc small.
Rory's feet
were big.

Skrekie squeezed his
four feet into Rory's boots.

At last, Skrekie was ready.

The two boys sneaked out of the back door.

When they arrived, Rory saw Skrekie staring at the playing field.

Skrekie stared at the visiting team.

Rory kept out of sight. Skrekie ran on to the field at the last moment. Mr. Mint didn't notice anything strange.

He started the game.

Chapter 6

Skrekie ran rings around the team from Springfield. He scored four goals.

As soon as the game was over, Rory and Skrekie made their getaway. Back in Rory's room, they did a dance of victory.

Skrekie jumped and fell on the bed ...

and vanished.

Rory's mom put her head in the door.

Mr. Mint was all smiles.

Mr. Mint went away, and Rory ran upstairs. He just had to tell Skrekie what had happened.

He could jump onto his quilt and into the future for just a minute ...

but the quilt wasn't there.

His mom had just emptied the washing machine.

Rory shrugged. He wouldn't be doing any more time travel, that was for sure.

About the author

Scoular Anderson is a popular author and illustrator. After studying graphic design at the Glasgow School of Art, he worked as an art teacher in Scotland.

Look for More *Read-It!* Chapter Books

Bricks for Breakfast by Julia Donaldson

Duncan and the Pirates by Peter Utton

Hetty the Yeti by Dee Shulman

Spookball Champions by Scoular Anderson

Toby and His Old Tin Tub by Colin West

Looking for a specific title or level? A complete list of *Read-it!* Chapter Books is available on our Web site: **www.picturewindowbooks.com**